JR. CHAPTER BOOK

THE
BAILEY SCHOOL
KIDS

JR. CHAPTER BOOK

THE
BAILEY SCHOOL
KIDS

VAMPIRES DO HUNT MARSHMALLOW BUNNIES

by Marcia Thornton Jones and Debbie Dadey
Illustrated by Joëlle Dreidemy

SCHOLASTIC INC.
New York Toronto London Auckland Sydney
Mexico City New Delhi Hong Kong Buenos Aires

To Hannah Rosenfeld—keep writing those stories!
—M.T.J.

To Brenton from Australia, Kevin, and Kevin,
and all the other kids who make my Web site so special.
Thanks for writing in and reading my books.
—D.D.

To my friends Lirim and Magali,
who don't like vampires very much...but
who LOVE candies indeed!
—J.D.

ISBN - 13: 978-0-545-03334-3
ISBN - 10: 0-545-03334-9

Text copyright © 2008 by Marcia Thornton Jones and Debra S. Dadey
Illustrations copyright © 2008 by Scholastic Inc.
All rights reserved. Published by Scholastic Inc.

SCHOLASTIC, THE BAILEY SCHOOL KIDS, and associated logos are
trademarks and/or registered trademarks of Scholastic Inc.

12 11 10 9 8 7   10 11 12 13/0

Printed in the U.S.A.
First printing, March 2008

CONTENTS

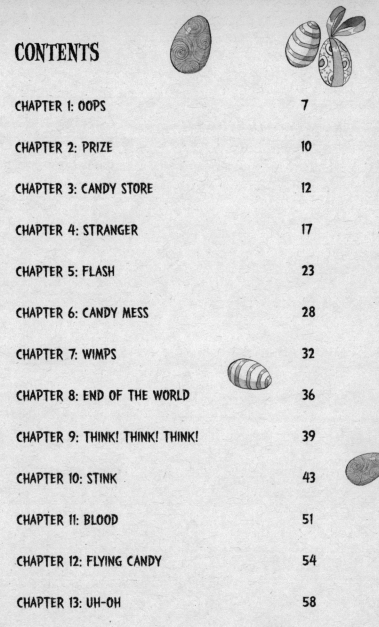

1

OOPS!

"Look out!" yelled Eddie.
A purple-and-green egg
soared past Melody's ear.
It flew by Howie. Splat! It
landed right on Liza's head.

She jumped.
She shook. And
then she screamed.
Yellow-and-
white egg slime
rolled down Liza's
face. "Yuck!" cried
Liza.

"Eddie, why
did you throw
an egg at Liza?"
Melody shouted.

Eddie held
up a basket filled
with colored eggs.
"I didn't mean
to hit her. I was
practicing."

"Practicing what?" asked Melody.

"Hiding eggs for the egg hunt tomorrow," said Eddie.

Howie handed Liza a tissue from his jacket pocket. She wiped off her face, but some yellow goop still sat on top of her blonde hair. "Eddie," Howie said, "don't you know that you're supposed to cook the eggs before you color them?"

2

PRIZE

"Oops," Eddie said. "I knew I forgot something." Melody put her hands on her hips. "Anyway, the Bailey City mayor will hide the eggs for the egg hunt, and he is hiding plastic eggs filled with candy. Not real eggs."

"Now we're talking," Eddie said, jumping up and down. Eddie loved candy almost as much as he loved sports.

"That's right," Howie said. "It was in the paper this

morning. One egg will hold a marshmallow bunny. Whoever finds that egg will win one hundred dollars!"

"Wow!" Melody said.
"Cool!" Liza said.
"Don't get too excited," Eddie said, jerking a thumb at his chest. "Because I'm going to find that marshmallow bunny!"

3
CANDY STORE

"All this talk of candy is making me hungry. I can't wait until tomorrow. Let's go to the candy store," Melody suggested. "I have my allowance."

Liza nodded. "I can clean this egg out of my hair in the bathroom at the store."

Eddie didn't say no. Eddie didn't say yes. He just ran as fast as he could to the candy store.

Liza, Melody, and Howie

followed him down the block to Dover's Five and Dime. Eddie zoomed around the corner and ran splat into a wall.

"Ouch!" Eddie said. "Who put this wall in front of Dover's?"

Eddie looked up. It wasn't a wall at all. Eddie had run into the tallest woman he'd ever seen.

"Excuse my friend, "Melody said to the woman. "We were just going to get some candy."

"Marshmallow bunnies," Eddie said with a grin. "I'm going to stuff my mouth with them."

The tall lady turned around. She opened her red lips in a big smile. Liza gasped when she saw the stranger's large pointy teeth.

"Greetings," the lady said.
"My name is Carmella Bitem
and I like ze candy, too. In fact,
I vill do just about anyzing to get
more of ze candy. And I mean
anyzing!"

4

STRANGER

Carmella Bitem's face was as white as an eggshell, but her clothes were black, black, black. Her hair was black, even her fingernails were black.

"If you like candy," Howie told her, "then I have good news for you."

Liza knew they shouldn't be talking to a stranger. She put her fingers to her lips. She made funny faces. Liza jumped up and down. She tried to get Howie to look at her. But Howie acted like Liza was a giant fly buzzing in the air.

The stranger put her face close to Howie's. "Tell me," she said. "Tell me everyzing zat you know."

Howie didn't blink. His eyes got bigger and bigger. He didn't look away.

"Everyzing, I mean, everything that I know?" he asked.

"Everyzing," Carmella repeated with a nod.

Howie spoke in a low, low voice. He sounded sleepy. Very sleepy.

"Earth is the third planet from the sun. Earth has one moon. The moon doesn't really shine. It reflects the sun. The sun is really a star. It is the closest star to Earth...."

"Snap out of it." Eddie clapped his hands in front of Howie's face. "This isn't science class."

"Howie knows a lot," Melody told the stranger. "If we didn't stop him, he could go on forever."

Howie blinked. He looked at his three friends. Then he stared at the strange woman in front of him. Liza looked at her, too. Only Liza didn't just stand there. She backed away. Step by step.

"Who ARE you?" Eddie asked the lady.

Carmella Bitem smiled. This time all the kids noticed her sharp eyeteeth. "I just flew into your town for a visit. But it is so nice, perhaps I vill stay. Forever."

5
FLASH

In a flash, the stranger was gone.

"That was one weird lady," Eddie said.

Howie nodded his head. "I felt like I was in a dream."

"You looked like a sleepwalker," Liza told him.

"Or a zombie," Eddie said.

"I think you were in a trance," Melody said.

"What did that lady do to you?" Liza asked. "Maybe we should tell the police about her."

"Or the mayor," Melody agreed.

"I think we should call the air force, the army, the navy, and the marines!" Eddie added.

Howie stomped his foot. "We don't have to tell anyone because I'm fine. But one thing is for sure, I'm staying away from Carmella Bitem. She's scary."

Liza nodded. Her voice shook when she spoke. "You're right. She looked like someone from a horror movie," she said, even though she had never actually seen a horror movie. Monsters scared Liza.

NOW PLAYING
Carmella Bitem in "VAMPIRES DO HUNT MARSHMALLOW BUNNIES"
3:00 6:00 9:00

Eddie thought a minute. "Carmella Bitem did have long, pointy teeth just like a vampire."

"And she talked like the most famous vampire of all," Howie said. "Count Dracula!"

"Don't be silly," Melody said. "There aren't really such things as vampires. Are there?"

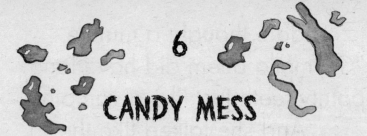

6

CANDY MESS

"Who cares about Carmella Bitem?" asked Eddie. "I want some candy."

The kids raced into the store. Liza wiped her hair off in the bathroom, and met her friends in the candy aisle. They didn't look happy.

"What's going on?" Liza asked.

"This is terrible!" Eddie said.

"It's a candy mess!" Howie cried out.

The friends stood in front of the jelly beans and marshmallow bunnies. Something was wrong. Very wrong.

The candy was tiny. And brown.

"It looks like someone sucked all the sugar right out of the candy," Melody said.

"Don't be silly," Howie told her.

Liza picked up a bag of candy. She held it close to get a better look. She looked at another bag. Three. Four. Five. She looked at six bags of candy.

"What are you doing?" Melody asked.

Liza's hand shook as she looked to the right. Then to the left. No one else was around, but she whispered anyway.

"I think Melody is right," Liza said. "Someone sucked the sugar right out of this candy. And I think Carmella Bitem did it!"

SHHH

"That's crazy," Howie said.

"You're nuts," Eddie said, grabbing a bag of marshmallow bunnies from the shelf. The bunnies were brown and all dried up.

"If you don't believe me, then look," Liza said. She pointed to two holes in the bag. "They're a perfect fit for fangs," she said. "Vampire fangs!"

7

WIMPS

"Maybe
Carmella Bitem
really IS a vampire,"
whispered Howie.
His face got white.
His eyes got wide.
He shook all over.

Melody's knees
shook. Then her arms
shook. Pretty soon she
shook all over, too.

"Are you okay?" Liza
asked her friends.

"They're wimps," Eddie said. He didn't look scared at all. In fact, Eddie smiled. "Vampires are cool."

Liza shook her head. "Ruining all the candy is not cool. What if Carmella does that at every store?"

Eddie stopped smiling. "This is not funny," he said. "We'd better check out the candy store at the mall."

Liza nodded. "I'll ask my mom to take us." The kids ran to Liza's house. Twenty minutes later, they were at the mall's candy store, staring at the closed sign.

"Why are you closed?" Melody asked the worker who was locking the door.

"It's the craziest thing," the candy store worker said. "One minute all our candy was fine. Then next, it was all brown and yucky."

Liza gasped. "Did you see a tall lady wearing a long, black dress?"

"How did you know?" the

worker asked.

Liza didn't know what to say. Neither did Howie and Melody. Eddie did though. He yelled, "It's the end of the world!"

8
END OF THE WORLD

"It's not the end of the world. We can live without candy," Melody told Eddie.

"Maybe you can," Eddie said. "But I can't."

"Don't worry," Howie said. "I'm sure there's plenty of candy left at the grocery store."

Eddie grinned. "Now you're talking. Liza, will your mom take us there on the way home?"

"I'll ask," Liza said.

Ten minutes later, the kids stood in front of the candy section of the grocery store.

It's horrible! | It's a disaster! | I can't believe it!

"That vampire lady has hunted down every last marshmallow bunny, every last jelly bean, and every last chocolate egg. She's sucked the sugar right out of all of them," Eddie said. He sat down on the floor with his head in his hands.

Eddie looked up. "We have to find Carmella Bitem and make her stop."

"She could be anywhere," Howie said. "She could be in Africa by now. Or Paris. Or outer space."

Eddie put his hands on his hips and cried. "Then we'll have to go to Africa. Or Paris. Or outer space. We have to find her!"

9

THINK! THINK! THINK!

"We can't," Liza said. "We're not allowed to ride buses alone."

"Or planes," Melody added.

"And especially not rocket ships," Howie said. "We're doomed to live in a candy-less world."

"What's even worse," Liza said, "is that without candy the egg hunt will be ruined."

Eddie's face turned as pale as an eggshell. "Maybe they'll use real eggs."

"But there won't be an egg filled with a marshmallow bunny," Melody said.

"And that means nobody will win the money," Howie added.

At that, Eddie exploded. Well, he didn't REALLY explode. But his face turned bright red. He jumped up and down. He flapped his arms.

NOoooo

Eddie put his nose up close to Howie's. "You're the smartest kid in Bailey City," Eddie said. "There MUST be something we can do. Think! Think! Think! How can we stop a sugar-sucking vampire from stealing our candy and ruining our egg hunt?"

Melody, Liza, and Eddie waited while Howie thought and thought and thought.

Then he thought some more.

All of a sudden, Howie smiled. His smile grew bigger and bigger and bigger. He snapped his fingers. "I've got it!" he said.

10

STINK

"THIS was your idea?"
Eddie asked Howie the next
day.

Howie held three necklaces
out to his friends. A fourth
hung from his neck. The string
necklaces had strange balls tied
on them. "It's the perfect way
to solve a vampire problem,"
Howie said.

"But it STINKS!" Liza said,
holding hers.

Howie rolled his eyes. "Of course it smells," he said. "It's garlic. But vampires can't stand it. I read it in a book.

"Believe me, if we wear these no vampire will dare come close." Howie added.

Eddie thought for a minute. "My Great Aunt Matilda wouldn't even kiss me if I wore this," he said.

Eddie quickly grabbed a
necklace and put it on.
Liza looked at Melody. Melody
made a face at the strings of
garlic. "Are you sure?" she
asked Howie.

Howie nodded. "I'm sure."
Melody and Liza put the
necklaces over their heads. A
cloud of garlic followed them
inside the store.

"I saw a truck deliver more candy this morning," Howie explained. "The shelves are full. All we have to do is stay near the candy until the mayor comes and buys the candy for the hunt. Thanks to us, the egg hunt will be saved."

Melody, Liza, and Eddie didn't have a better plan, so there was only one thing for

EASTER CAND

them to do. They followed Howie to the candy aisle.

Howie was right. The shelves were full of colorful candy eggs and pink and yellow marshmallow bunnies. Eddie's mouth watered at the sight of them.

The kids marched up and down the aisle, guarding the bunnies.

A woman with a cart turned down the aisle. She stopped. She sniffed. "Pee-yew!" she said and hurried away.

A man with a basket headed toward the bunnies. He stopped. He sniffed. "Pee-yew!" he said and rushed off.

All the shoppers stopped
dead in their tracks. Their faces
turned green. They held their
noses. They ran away shrieking.

"My plan is working," Howie said.

But just then a dark shadow appeared at the end of the aisle. Eddie turned as pale as a marshmallow. Liza shook. "Uh-oh," she said with a gulp.

11

BLOOD

Big pointy teeth. Dripping red blood. That's all Liza saw. She screamed and fainted.

Melody held out her necklace. "You stay away from us," she told Carmella Bitem.

"I just vanted to get ze candy," Carmella said.

She sipped
the last of her
tomato juice
and dropped
it in a nearby
trash can.

"Vat about
ze friend of
yours?" the pale lady asked.
"Is she all right?"

Howie nodded. "She's fine.
You just scared her."

"Oh my," the stranger said.
"I do not like to frighten ze
children. Children are...sveet."
And then Carmella smiled
and showed them her pointy
eyeteeth.

Eddie whispered. "Sweet, sure, she likes to suck their blood."

The lady took one step toward the kids. "Stay back," Melody said. "We aren't supposed to talk to strangers."

But the lady took another step. And another.

12

FLYING CANDY

"Ready. Aim. Fire!" Melody threw a bag of marshmallow bunnies at Carmella Bitem.

Eddie grabbed more candy bags. He tossed them in the air.

"It's raining bunnies!" Liza said, sitting up on the floor.

"We're fighting off the candy-vampire," Howie told Liza. He grabbed a bag of marshmallow bunnies. He flung them toward Carmella.

Carmella smiled and caught one of the bags of bunnies. She stuck her teeth in the bag and sucked all the bunnies until they turned brown.

"This isn't helping," Melody said. "She likes the candy."

"Throw the garlic," Howie suggested. The four kids flung their necklaces toward the candy vampire.

"Ahhhh-chew!" sneezed Carmella. "Zis is a crazy place," she yelled and dropped the bunnies. She backed away from the garlic and frowned at the four kids. "You aren't sveet at all!"

"This is Bailey City," Eddie said. "Kids are different here."

"Too different," Carmella said. "I vill not stay here. I zink zis is not ze right place for me."

And then Carmella Bitem disappeared.

Liza jumped up and down. "We did it! We got rid of the vampire!"

Just then another dark shadow appeared beside the kids. "What have you done?" the shadow yelled.

13

UH-OH

Melody's legs shook.
Howie dropped a bag of candy
while Liza hid behind Melody.
"Uh-oh," Eddie said. "I think
we're in big trouble."

Uh-oh...

The Bailey City mayor stood beside the candy shelf. Only most of the candy wasn't on the shelf. Most of the candy was on the floor. The mayor did not look happy. He rubbed his chin and asked, "Who made this mess?"

"Maybe it was a hungry teacher?" Melody said.

"Could it have been a windstorm?" Howie said.

"Would you believe monsters from outer space?" Eddie asked.

"No," said the mayor. "I believe it was a bunch of silly kids."

Liza came out from behind Melody. "We're sorry, Mayor. Believe it or not, we were saving the egg hunt."

"You're right. I find that hard to believe," said the mayor. "But you can start helping me now."

"We'll clean up this mess," Howie said. "And we can carry all the candy to your car for you."

"After you buy it, of course," Melody added.

The mayor smiled. "Now that sounds like the right kind of help."

"Don't forget to buy a marshmallow bunny!" cried Eddie.

"Maybe one of you will even win the prize in the egg hunt," added the mayor.

Eddie grinned. "I'm going to find the marshmallow bunny and eat it."

"What about the money?" the mayor asked.

Eddie's answer surprised his friends. "I'm going to share it with my friends."

"Really?" Liza asked.

Eddie nodded. "Really."

"Eddie just might be sweet after all," Howie said with a grin.

"And you know what that means, don't you?" Melody teased. "Eddie would make a perfect vampire treat!"

Eddie covered his throat with his hands. He looked up. He looked right. He looked left.

"Whew," Eddie said when he was sure the store was vampire-free.

Eddie and his friends headed out of the store.

"Don't worry," Howie said as he patted his friend on the shoulder. "Carmella Bitem's gone for now. But remember, you never know vat vill happen next in Bailey City!"